Dear Parents:

Congratulations! Your child is taking the first steps on an exciting journey. The destination? Independent reading!

STEP INTO READING® will help your child get there. The program offers five steps to reading success. Each step includes fun stories and colorful art or photographs. In addition to original fiction and books with favorite characters, there are Step into Reading Non-Fiction Readers, Phonics Readers and Boxed Sets, Sticker Readers, and Comic Readers—a complete literacy program with something to interest every child.

Learning to Read, Step by Step!

Ready to Read   Preschool–Kindergarten
• big type and easy words • rhyme and rhythm • picture clues
For children who know the alphabet and are eager to begin reading.

Reading with Help   Preschool–Grade 1
• basic vocabulary • short sentences • simple stories
For children who recognize familiar words and sound out new words with help.

Reading on Your Own   Grades 1–3
• engaging characters • easy-to-follow plots • popular topics
For children who are ready to read on their own.

Reading Paragraphs   Grades 2–3
• challenging vocabulary • short paragraphs • exciting stories
For newly independent readers who read simple sentences with confidence.

Ready for Chapters   Grades 2–4
• chapters • longer paragraphs • full-color art
For children who want to take the plunge into chapter books but still like colorful pictures.

STEP INTO READING® is designed to give every child a successful reading experience. The grade levels are only guides; children will progress through the steps at their own speed, developing confidence in their reading.

Remember, a lifetime love of reading starts with a single step!

Copyright © 2022 Disney Enterprises, Inc. All rights reserved. Published in the United States by Random House Children's Books, a division of Penguin Random House LLC, 1745 Broadway, New York, NY 10019, and in Canada by Penguin Random House Canada Limited, Toronto, in conjunction with Disney Enterprises, Inc.

Step into Reading, Random House, and the Random House colophon are registered trademarks of Penguin Random House LLC.

Visit us on the Web!
StepIntoReading.com
rhcbooks.com

Educators and librarians, for a variety of teaching tools, visit us at RHTeachersLibrarians.com

ISBN 978-0-7364-4308-1 (trade) — ISBN 978-0-7364-9027-6 (lib. bdg.)
ISBN 978-0-7364-4309-8 (ebook)

Printed in the United States of America

10 9 8 7 6 5 4 3 2 1

Disney

MONSTERS
AT WORK

Little Monsters

Adapted by Nicole Johnson

Based on the original screenplay by
Ricky Roxburgh and Bobs Gannaway

Random House 🏠 New York

4

It is Mini Monsters Day
at Monsters, Inc.!
All the monsters bring
their kids to work with them.
The little monsters get to learn
about different jobs at
the company.

One little monster, Thalia,
is not happy.
Thalia does not like
Mini Monsters Day.
Her mom is Ms. Flint.
Ms. Flint hires Jokesters.

Thalia is not excited

to be stuck

with the MIFT group

for the day.

She thinks it will be boring.

She joins the other Mini Monsters

in the MIFT group.

Tylor is not excited, either.

He just had another bad

Jokester Audition.

Ms. Flint said he was not funny.

Val tries to make him feel better.

"No one can be sad on

Mini Monsters Day!" she says.

Each Mini Monster gets
paired with a MIFTer.
Thalia is paired with Val.

Tylor wants to make Thalia laugh.

He thinks she will tell her mom

how funny he is.

Then he can be a Jokester!

"Trade with me?" Tylor says to Val.

Val agrees.

But Thalia does not like Tylor.
She knows what he is doing.
Scarers always tried to impress
Thalia because of who her mom is.
They do not treat her
like a friend.

Fritz soon gets a work order
from Smitty and Needleman.

Their baby ran away!

"This is as bad as when we lost the kid last year," Needleman says.

"And the year before that," Smitty adds.

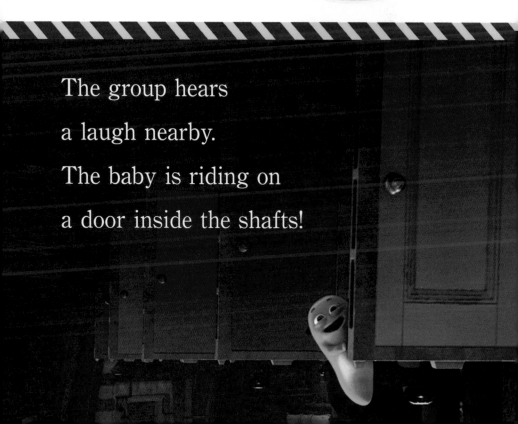

The group hears a laugh nearby. The baby is riding on a door inside the shafts!

The MIFTers take off after him!
They ride in carts to search
the doors.

They zoom around the door shafts,

but they keep missing the baby.

Tylor and Thalia almost crash!

Fritz sees the baby

on a security camera.

It is heading toward

a door shredder!

16

Tylor and Thalia are close by.

They rush over.

Thalia takes control of the cart.

Tylor jumps onto the door

and grabs the baby.

They have saved the day!

The team cheers

for Tylor and Thalia.

"Good job, everyone!"
Fritz says.
Thalia is happy.
She is having a fun time
with MIFT after all!

But then Tylor tries to tell
her another joke.
"You are not funny," she says.
Thalia is unhappy again.
She thought Tylor was her friend.
Now she feels like he only
cares about becoming a Jokester.

Tylor complains to Val.
"Thalia can go find her mom
and tell her *she* is the most
unfunny monster in all of
Monstropolis, not me!" he says.

Tylor turns around.

Thalia is there.

Oops.

"I'll go tell her that," she says,

and leaves the MIFT office.

"Wait!" Tylor shouts.

He regrets what he said.

He hops into a cart

to catch Thalia.

But she is already

in the elevator.

Tylor rushes upstairs.

The floor is slimey.

The cart slips and slides.

CRASH!

Tylor runs into a coffee stand.

He is covered in treats.

Tylor hears something surprising.

The monsters around him

are laughing—even Thalia!

Tylor apologizes to her.
"I was trying to make you laugh
so your mom would make me
a Jokester," he says.
"But that was wrong."

Thalia forgives Tylor because
he was brave enough to admit
his mistake.
They shake hands and make up.

Thalia and Tylor go back to MIFT.

Fritz gives a speech.

"I'm so proud of each and every
one of you," he says.

"I'm proud to be
a Mini MIFTer!"
says Thalia.

The little monsters cheer.

"M-I-F-T!" they chant

as they go back to their parents.

Later, Thalia tells her mom
about her day with Tylor.
"He was really funny," she says.
Ms. Flint looks surprised.
Maybe Tylor will get another
chance after all!